iHorror

STEVE BARLOW ✦ STEVE SKIDMORE

VAMPIRE
HUNTER

iHorror

VAMPIRE HUNTER

Steve Barlow
&
Steve Skidmore

Illustrated by
Paul Davidson

ORCHARD BOOKS

ORCHARD BOOKS
338 Euston Road, London NW1 3BH
Orchard Books Australia
Level 17/207 Kent St, Sydney, NSW 2000

A Paperback Original
First published in Great Britain in 2011

A CIP catalogue record for this book is available from
the British Library.

ISBN 978 1 40830 985 8

1 3 5 7 9 10 8 6 4 2

Printed in Great Britain

The paper and board used in this paperback are natural recyclable
products made from wood grown in sustainable forests. The
manufacturing processes conform to the environmental regulations of
the country of origin.

Orchard Books is a division of Hachette Children's Books,
an Hachette UK company

www.hachette.co.uk

*"You better watch out,
unless you want to die."*

Victoria Boatwright

iHorror

There is a dark, unseen world around us, of
supernatural horrors beyond our imagination.
Sometimes the worlds of humans and horrors
collide, threatening our very existence.

In iHorror, you make decisions that will affect
how the story unfolds. Each section of this book is
numbered. At the end of most sections, you will have
to make a choice. The choice you make will take you
to a different section of the book.

Some of your choices will help you to complete the
adventure successfully. But choose wisely. Make the
wrong choice and you could end up dead!

Dare you enter the world of iHorror?
Fight your fear. Choose your fate...

Who is the Hunter?

You are the Hunter, protecting the world of humans from supernatural horrors in all their forms. Vampires, werewolves, demons, zombies – you have fought all these creatures and more, and you've always beaten them... so far.

Over more years than you can remember you have become an expert in martial arts, including Jujitsu, Wing Chun and Taekwondo. You have amassed a store of weapons for every occasion: from ancient, magical daggers to ultra-modern, rapid fire guns – including some that fire mini wooden stakes for hunting vampires. Whatever it takes to defeat the creatures of the dark, you will use.

Prepare to face your latest test in Vampire Hunter.

And so it begins...

It is a cold, dark January evening and you have received news that a vampire has arrived in London, seeking new blood for the new year. Using your expertise in hunting down supernatural creatures, you have tracked the vampire across the city to its lair – an old, abandoned London tube train station. Armed with a flamer that shoots jets of fire and a gun that fires wooden bullets for shooting vampires through their undead hearts, you make your way to your date with the vampire.

‡ *Go to 1.*

1

It is dusk and snow is falling as you arrive at the underground station in your SUV. You step out of your vehicle and shiver – not with cold but at the thought of what you will have to face in the coming hours. Above you, the outline of a full moon hangs in the darkening sky. "Just right for vampire hunting," you mutter to yourself. Your feet crunch on the recently fallen snow as you make your way to the metal shuttered door of the station. To your surprise it is open – perhaps someone, or rather something, is expecting you...

You step inside the abandoned station. It is pitch black so you activate your night-vision goggles. The goggles cut through the dark and you see several fat rats running around. But you're here for pest control of the undead kind. You move across the ticket hall and see two signs pointing to different sets of stairs.

One reads, "To the service tunnel" and the other, "To the platform".

- ‡ *To go down the service tunnel stairway, go to 49.*
- ‡ *To head towards the platform, go to 90.*
- ‡ *To investigate the ticket hall, go to 32.*

2

You shoot at the nightmarish creature. The bullets
rip into its body and it drops to the floor with a
deafening scream. At the same moment, the bats
in the cellar also drop to the floor – the cellar is a
writhing mass. You rush over to the vampire. You are
amazed – it is still alive! The creature lies on the floor,
uttering threats and twisting its body as it tries to
claw at you.

‡ *If you want to question the creature,*
  go to 71.
‡ *If you wish to use your flamer, go to 20.*
‡ *If you wish to shoot it, go to 45.*

3

You throw the petrol can onto the fire and dive back through the doorway.

There is an explosion, and a ball of fire and smoke engulfs the room. Bats and vampires burst into flames, their death screams cut through the air. The surviving vampires try to get out of the room, but you are ready for them and your aim is true. The air fills with ash.

The fireball dies down and there is silence.

- ⁑ *If you wish to go back into the room, go to 52.*
- ⁑ *If you want to wait to see if any more vampires emerge from the room, go to 40.*

3: The vampires are caught in the ball of flame.

4

The vampires attack! Bowling balls and pins hurtle towards you but all the reflexes you have developed in your martial arts training help you dodge them easily. You wonder if that's the best they can do.

As you spin away you begin shooting at the vampires. Your aim is good and several of the creatures are quickly dispatched. You leap over the counter and deal with the two vampires there. As the remaining vampires move in, you see an open door leading to a kitchen.

‡ *To go through the door, go to 94.*
‡ *If you wish to continue the fight, go to 92.*

5

You move cautiously further into the depths of the cellar, heading towards the fuse box that controls the mansion's electricity supply. You listen for the sound of any movement, but hear nothing.

You reach the fuse box and quickly reset the lights and security system. As you turn to leave the cellar, again you hear wings flapping. Your heart beats faster as you see a dark shape flash across the cellar and brush against your hair. You turn to flick it away, but instantly the air is filled with more black shapes.

Another wingtip brushes against your head. This is followed by another and another. The cellar is full of bats!

    ‡ *If you decide to explore the cellar, go to 34.*
    ‡ *If you wish to leave the cellar, go to 54.*

6

You head into the service tunnel, which is small and cramped. Electric wires line the walls and you can hear the faint hum of machinery in the distance.

You slowly make your way along the passageway, pausing every few steps to listen for any suspicious noise. Sweat drips from your forehead as the air in the tunnel becomes hot and stale. You instinctively sense danger, something that only comes with your years of experience hunting the creatures of the dark. Your heart beats faster as adrenaline rushes around your body. This would be a bad place to be attacked.

Ahead of you is a side opening with stairs leading down. You read a fading sign on the wall. It says "To the platform".

    ‡ *To take these stairs, go to 90.*
    ‡ *To continue your way along the tunnel, go to 37.*

7

Holding your loaded gun, you make your way up the stairs, listening for any suspicious noises. Your heart beats faster as you take each step.

Eventually you reach a landing at the top of the stairway. On the left there is another set of steps leading up to the penthouse suite and on the right there is a door, from behind which you can hear music and the chatter of voices.

‡ *If you'd like to open the door, go to 51.*
‡ *If you want to head up to the penthouse suite, go to 95.*

8

You step out of the tube station. The full moon shines down, lighting up the snow-covered ground. Large snowflakes swirl around as you step into your SUV. You type in the address of the bowling alley into your satnav.

You wipe away the grime of the underground tunnel from your face and replenish your ammunition before driving to the bowling alley. It is situated in a run-down part of the city. You drive past the entrance to the alley. A neon sign above the door flickers on and off adding to the gloom of the evening.

KNOCK 'EM DEAD
ALL NIGHT
BOWLING ALLEY

You park across the road and stake out the building for some time. During that period, you see no one entering or leaving the bowling alley. You decide to investigate inside.

- ⚘ *To look for a back entrance into the building, go to 96.*
- ⚘ *If you decide to go in through the front entrance, go to 30.*

9

Still holding the vampire's cloak, you dive for the UV grenade and pick it up.

"Goodbye," you say. "You've been a pain in the neck for too long."

The vampire smiles, revealing its wicked-looking fangs. "If you detonate that, you will blind yourself."

"Not if I can cover my eyes with something that won't let the rays through."

"Did you bring your sunglasses on this vacation?" laughs the vampire.

"I didn't need to, I've got this." You hold up the cloak. "Good for keeping the sun off!"

The vampire screams and flies at you. With one movement, you cover your eyes with the cloak and detonate the UV grenade. Instantly, the room fills with an intense light. You hear screams, then there is silence. The light fades and you take the cloak from your eyes. The room is empty – nothing remains of the vampire. You have defeated it!

As you stand savouring your victory, the castle begins to shake. You look up at the picture above the fireplace – it seems to be moving! Ceiling beams begin to crash down and the walls start to crack. You have to get out of this place!

‡ *To head for the doorway, go to 93.*
‡ *To head towards the fireplace, go to 73.*

10

You reach for your flamer, but it snags on your belt and the vampire is at your throat.

You try desperately to beat off the attack, but the creature is powerful. You can smell its breath – it is the smell of death. Just as it is about to sink its teeth into your neck, you swing your elbow up into its chin and the vampire staggers back. You have gained a few precious seconds, but you know that you don't have time to untangle your flamer...

‡ *To reach for your gun, go to 59.*
‡ *To fight it using your martial arts skills, go to 98.*

11

You climb onto the top of the elevator before
reaching into your bag and pulling out a rope and
climbing ascender. You attach it to the elevator's steel
cable and use it to pull yourself up the cable.

Your muscles strain as you inch your way further
up the cable. As you do so, you wonder why the
vampire wants to meet you here. Snow continues to
fall and the bright lights of Paris twinkle far below.
Eventually, you reach the final level of the Eiffel
Tower and step out onto the platform. You reach
into your bag and pull out your gun ready for what
is to come...

Mr Pavie is waiting for you. "Welcome, Hunter,"
he says. "I can tell that you are wondering why I
wanted you to come here." He spreads his cloaked
arm out and gestures at the snow-filled black sky.
"Look out at this miserable world of humankind.
In sprawling cities like this across the planet live
millions of people – lost in greed, selfishness and
hatred. Wars, famine, poverty – all caused because of
human actions."

He turns back to you and, in a voice that seems to
touch your very soul, continues to talk. "My master is
the only one who can bring back order to this dying
planet. You have been against us for too long, he
wishes you to join with us and help us supernatural

creatures rule this world. Think of what we could
create together – rid this sickly world of the weak,
the poor, the miserable..."

He smiles, his fangs shining in the moonlight.
"What do you say, Hunter?"

‡ *If you wish to ignore Mr Pavie and shoot him
immediately, go to 28.*
‡ *If you would rather keep the vampire talking,
go to 23.*

12

You head to the cellar door. You start to move down
the stone steps holding your gun at the ready. Even
with your night-vision goggles on there are shadows
that are deep and black. Your breathing becomes
heavier and your heart beats faster in anticipation of
what is to come.

Suddenly, you hear the beating of wings and the
cellar is filled with brilliant light. You cry out in pain
as the white light flares in your eyes and dazzles you.

‡ *If you wish to fire your gun, go to 89.*
‡ *If you decide to take off your goggles, go to 76.*

13

You turn the handle and push – the door is unlocked.
With your gun ready, you step into a gloomy corridor,
which is lit by a single bulb dangling from the ceiling.
You can hear the sound of bowling coming from the
bowling alley – dull thuds and cheers.

As you make your way down the corridor a wild-
eyed man steps out of a door and smashes you on the
head with a heavy wooden bowling pin. As you crash
to the floor he says calmly, "Hi! I'm the staff and I
knock 'em dead!" Then the world goes black.

‡ *Go to 70.*

14

"I'd like to book a room," you tell the receptionist. "Just for a night."

The receptionist nods and hands you a key for room 101. "It is on the tenth floor," she tells you. She has a strange look in her eyes and her voice is strained.

You thank her before nonchalantly saying, "Oh, I have a friend staying at the hotel. His name is Mr Pavie. What's the number of his room?"

The receptionist stares at you. "Mr Pavie lives in the penthouse suite. Shall I tell him you are here?"

"No, I'll surprise him," you reply.

As you head towards the elevator, you hear the receptionist pick up a phone. Although she speaks quietly, you can just make out some of her conversation. "Here at last... Hunter... trap..."

You grip your bag tightly and look around, readying yourself for any attack. But it doesn't come, so you take the elevator to the tenth floor and are soon in your room, loading your weapons. You take a gun, your flamer, the UV grenade and night-vision goggles. You leave your room and head across the landing to the elevators and the staircase that both lead to the penthouse suite at the top of the hotel.

‡ *If you want to take the elevator, go to 17.*
‡ *If you want to take the stairs, go to 7.*

15

Just in time, you leap up onto the platform. As you do an underground train hurtles by, lights blazing.

As it passes by the force of the air nearly knocks you off your feet. You totter on the edge of the platform, desperately trying to stop yourself falling onto the track. Luckily your martial arts training has given you superb reflexes and balance. You regain your footing and give a sigh of relief.

Wiping the sweat of fear from your brow, you head along the platform where you see a door marked

DANGER
DO NOT ENTER!

You try to open it, but it is locked.

‡ *If you wish to use your flamer on the lock, go to 43.*
‡ *If you wish to return to the tunnel, go to 72.*

16

The bats fly at you, but you easily brush them aside.
You shoot at one or two, obliterating them into a
mass of blood and fur, and the attack soon subsides.

As you move further into the cellar, you see a
movement behind a large barrel. You move forward
cautiously, gun held out. "Come out, come out,
whatever you are," you say.

Suddenly, there is a scream. A woman dressed in
white robes flies out at you, teeth bared in a terrifying
grimace of hatred.

> ‡ *To use the UV grenade, go to 56.*
> ‡ *To shoot the vampire, go to 2.*
> ‡ *To use your martial arts fighting skills, go to 98.*

17

You press the elevator button. To your surprise, the
doors immediately open – as if it was waiting for you!
You step inside the elevator and lean against the wall
– it is covered in a black, leathery material.

The door slams shut and the elevator begins its
journey.

Suddenly you give a startled cry – the walls are
closing in on you! Sharp talons appear and your blood
turns to ice as you realise that the walls of the lift

16: A vampire dressed in white robes flies at you.

are, in reality, the wings of a giant bat! The leathery wings close in on you, crushing your body in a deadly vice-like grip.

In desperation you manage to reach for your gun and shoot at the wing, tearing a small hole in the membrane. The bat releases its grip and you plunge your fist into the hole and rip at it. There is a deafening screech and the bat transforms into human form. Its left arm hangs helplessly at its side.

The vampire points at you. "The smell of human blood – so invigorating!" it says. "And your veins are so full of it." With a roar of hatred, the creature leaps at you.

‡ *To shoot the vampire, go to 98.*
‡ *To fight it in hand-to-hand combat, go to 61.*

18

You hide the UV grenade behind your back and reach for your gun with your other hand. Keeping a sharp eye on the other vampires, you shake your head. "I suppose you're going to ask me to become one of you," you say. "Save it – I'm not interested – I couldn't afford my dentist's bills."

The old vampire snarls. "You are a fool, Hunter. You are in my world now. You will become one of my followers, whether you choose to be so or not."

"I don't think so," you reply. "On account of this..."

‡ *If you want to threaten the vampire with the UV grenade, go to 33.*

‡ *If you wish to shoot the vampires with your gun, go to 60.*

‡ *If you want to detonate the UV grenade, go to 56.*

19

You turn right and walk down the platform. On your right you see a door marked "DANGER – DO NOT ENTER". You try to open it, but it is locked.

‡ *If you wish to use your flamer on the lock, go to 43.*

‡ *If you wish to make your way down the right-hand tunnel, go to 72.*

20

Using your flamer you torch the vampire where it lies
– its body quickly turning black. The creature of the
night releases a nightmarish scream before turning
into ash before your eyes. It is a sight you have seen
before and hope to see again very soon.

You check the cellar, but there is nothing else to
interest you here. You decide to head immediately to
the local airfield to fly your private plane to Paris for
a meeting with the enigmatic Mr Pavie.

‡ *Go to 58.*

21

Although you don't trust the vampire, you go along with its suggestion. "I give you my word," you say. "Tell me what you know."

The vampire hisses. "The Hunter is the hunted. You are wanted. Things are not what they seem."

You are puzzled. "What do you mean?" you ask.

"You'll never know," it snaps and with a demonic cry it leaps at you.

However, you were ready for the attack and you easily avoid the flying creature and send a volley of bullets crashing into its body. It drops to the floor and instantly turns to dust.

"I knew you'd do that," you say. "Never trust a vampire – one of the first things my old granny said to me."

You wonder what to do next – there are a lot more vampires that you will need to deal with, but you wonder who or what is directing them. You decide to head back to your mansion, to rearm and try and work out what the vampire meant by you being wanted and things not being as they seem.

‡ *Go to 50.*

22

You put your gun away and refill your flamer. You step towards the door and burst in.

There before you is a group of a dozen or so down-and-outs sitting in front of a small fire, which causes your night vision to flare and momentarily blind you. As your sight gradually returns, you see that the down-and-outs are staring at you.

You glance upwards and see that the roof is covered with bats, hanging upside down.

"Nobody move!" you shout. "I don't want to have to hurt you."

One of the figures stands up. "Oh you won't," he says. "Will he, my brothers and sisters?" As one they smile, each revealing a set of razor sharp fangs. Slowly, they get up and head towards you.

‡ *To use your flamer, go to 46.*
‡ *To try to escape, go to 77.*

23

"Who is this Master of yours, and where is he?" you ask, playing for time.

"In his lair, but not yet in this time or place, but he can be if you join us," replies the vampire. He steps forward slowly. "Join us, Hunter, and rise above humankind."

You slowly wrap your finger around the trigger of your gun and shake your head. "Maybe humans aren't all good, but they aren't all bad like vampires. No deal!"

With a single movement, you swing your gun up,

aim and fire. Mr Pavie is caught off guard and the
wooden bullet hits his shoulder. With a snarl of
rage, he leaps towards you and knocks you down.
As he does so, something black and shiny falls from
his pocket.

The vampire grapples with you, but you are equal
to his strength – with a twist of your body you send
him flying through the air. He regains his feet and as
he lunges forward again you shoot him through the
heart. Smoke fills his mouth and he shrieks in terror
as he realises what you've done. Then he explodes,
showering you with thick ash.

"Dust to dust," you mutter grimly. "Now to find out who this Master of yours is." Wiping your face, you wonder what Mr Pavie meant by "not yet in this time and place". As you turn to head back to the hotel, you see the object that Mr Pavie dropped – it is a mobile phone. You pick it up and scroll through some of the messages, but one about the penthouse catches your attention. It gives you the number of the access keycode!

You smile – these vampires may live forever, but they don't get any smarter. You head quickly back to the hotel.

‡ *Go to 69.*

24

You climb through the open window and make your way along the corridor to the flight of stairs. You head down the stairs and come to a landing, where there is a metal elevator door and a wooden door with a sign that reads "TO THE ROOF".

> ‡ *If you wish to head up to the roof, go to 13.*
> ‡ *If you wish to continue going down the stairs, go to 88.*
> ‡ *If you wish to use the elevator, go to 17.*

25

You head up to the penthouse but then, seeing the access keypad, realise you need Mr Pavie for the code. You curse your own stupidity – you will have to follow the vampire to the Eiffel Tower. You head to the elevators.

> ‡ *Go to 17.*

26

You stand in front of the picture and something
catches your eye – the picture seems to be moving!
Light flickers from the windows of the castle and the
trees seem to be moving in an invisible wind. You
recall what Mr Pavie said about his master – "Not yet
in this time or place."

You reach out and touch the painting. There
is a sudden explosion and you are sucked into a
maelstrom of wind and noise that sends you spinning
round and round.

In an instant the noise stops and you find yourself
standing in a huge stone hallway.

"Welcome to my castle, Hunter." You spin around to see an old, white-haired vampire standing on a winding staircase. Standing alongside him are more vampires. "I see that you found the entrance to my world." The old vampire points at a large picture hanging above a huge fireplace – it is identical to the one in the penthouse suite. As you unclip the UV grenade from your belt, the vampire speaks. "I am glad you are here, I have need of you."

‡ *If you wish to talk to the vampire, go to 18.*
‡ *If you wish to use the UV grenade immediately, go to 56.*

27

You drop down off the platform, making sure that you don't touch the rail track. You make your way into the entrance of the tunnel.

As you enter the tunnel, there is a rush of foul wind that nearly causes you to stagger onto the live rail track. You hear a roaring sound in the distance that gets louder by the second.

‡ *To carry on along the tunnel, go to 86.*
‡ *To climb back onto the platform, go to 15.*

28

Before you can fire your gun, Mr Pavie vanishes before your eyes. You look around, frantically. You can still hear his voice, but do not recognise the language. You know it is ancient and evil. You try to move but find your legs are too heavy. Your arms hang limply at your side as you drop your gun to the floor.

A feeling of weakness floods through your body; it is as though your soul is being dragged from your body. Mr Pavie appears in front of you but you are powerless to react.

The vampire steps closer and whispers in your ear. "You will join us, whether you like it or not," he says softly.

Many hours later, you wake up in a dark cellar. You realise that you are tied up in metal chains. Standing over you is a vampire with long, white hair and wrinkled skin.

You shiver with fear.

‡ *Go to 99.*

29

You decide to head to Paris, but will have to be very careful. The letter is your only clue, but it sounds like a trap.

You go to the marble fireplace and press a hidden button. The whole fireplace swings open to reveal your secret laboratory, where you keep your special weapons, designed to help you defeat the supernatural creatures you spend your life hunting.

You enter the lab and as the lights flicker on you put your night-vision goggles on a desk. You head towards the weapons store. There are a variety of guns, crossbows, silver bullets (for dealing with werewolves) and other deadly gadgets, including your latest weapon, an Ultra Violet grenade that emits a burst of intense UV light. You have been developing this weapon for using against vampires. The light from it is deadly against vampires. You know that it is a weapon of last resort – one that would blind you if you used it in an enclosed space, even if you have your eyes closed. You hope that you won't need it, but it is better to be prepared.

You pack a case with your equipment and weapons and head back into the study. As the fireplace closes, you hear a noise in the hallway. You take out your gun and rush through the door. The hallway is still

dark and empty, but there is light and noise now
coming from the cellar.

‡ *If you wish to investigate the cellar now you*
are fully armed, go to 97.
‡ *If you decide to sneak out and head for Paris,*
go to 82.

30

You make your way to the entrance of the Knock
'em Dead Bowling Alley and head into the lobby. The
young woman sitting at the pay desk looks up at you.

"What brings you here?" she asks.

The question surprises you. "I want to play a game
and knock 'em dead, of course."

She makes a low hissing sound. "Of course," she
replies.

"Not many people here this evening," you say as
you hand over payment.

"There's never many people here ever. And if there
are, they don't stay very long," she adds with a cruel
look in her eyes.

‡ *If you are suspicious of the woman, go to 79.*
‡ *If you wish to make your way towards the*
bowling lanes, go to 48.

31

"Could you tell Mr Pavie that I am here to see him," you say.

The receptionist raises an eyebrow and picks up the phone. She speaks quietly but you catch some of her words. "Here at last... Hunter... trap..."

You glance down at your bag containing your weapons to make sure it is open, just in case you need to use them. Finally she puts down the phone. "Mr Pavie will be pleased to see you – he is in the penthouse suite. You can take the elevator."

You thank her and head across the lobby towards the elevators. Next to the elevators is a staircase.

‡ *If you wish to take the elevator, go to 17.*
‡ *If you decide you will climb the stairs, go to 67.*

32

As you step forward you hear the noise of beating wings. You duck and spin round quickly as a vampire materialises before your eyes. In an instant, he leaps at you – his open mouth revealing sharp, wicked-looking fangs.

‡ *To use your gun, go to 59.*
‡ *To use your flamer, go to 10.*
‡ *To fight the vampire with your bare hands, go to 98.*

33

You pull out the UV grenade and hold it up. "If I pull this trigger, it's the end for all of you."

The vampires snarl with rage as the Master vampire steps forward.

"Perhaps so, but you too would suffer, I think..."

"That's a risk you'll have to take, isn't it?" you reply.

The old vampire's voice cuts through the air. It is soft and persuasive. "Hunter, think of what you would destroy. Just imagine the blood of the Hunter mixed with that of the vampire – we would be invincible." He holds out his hands beckoning you to join him... You feel your will draining away.

"Join us."

With a great effort, you shake your head and return

33: The Master vampire asks you to join him.

to your senses. "Never!"

"Then drain his body of blood, my children," orders the Master vampire.

With a scream, the other vampires fly at you.

✢ *To detonate the grenade, go to 56.*

✢ *To shoot at the vampires before they get too close, go to 87.*

34

Suddenly from out of the cloud of bats, the outline of a man emerges. You get a brief glimpse of the figure, and realise it is another vampire!

Before you can react, the creature moves across the cellar at lightning speed, grabs you around the throat and lifts you from the floor. Your gun is knocked from your hand as the creature tightens its grip. You can feel its hot breath on your neck.

"So, Hunter, what does it feel like to be caught?" the creature whispers into your ear. Its grip on your throat tightens, slowly cutting off your air supply. You try to fight back, but it is hopeless. You feel a burst of

agonising pain as the creature's teeth rip into your flesh and slowly suck your precious blood from your body.

> ‡ *You have been defeated and paid the ultimate price. To begin again, go to 1.*

35

You reach the snow-covered flat rooftop of the building. You look around and see a glass skylight, which you smash open with your foot.

As you drop down through the skylight, you catch your hand on a jagged piece of glass. Blood drips from the wound. The building is suddenly filled with a chorus of screeching and howling, which then stops as quickly as it began.

You have dropped into a narrow corridor, which winds round to a flight of stairs. You make your way down the stairs and come to a landing, where you see an elevator door.

> ‡ *If you wish to carry on down the stairs, go to 88.*
> ‡ *If you wish to take the elevator, go to 17.*

36

"Of course I do," you reply. "You are vampire – it is an anagram of Mr Pavie. Not very subtle."

Mr Pavie smiles, revealing his deadly fangs. "Perhaps not, but I know who you are – you are the Hunter. I've so wanted to meet you and so does my master..." He steps forward, but before he can attack, you reach into your bag and pull out the UV grenade. "If I pull this trigger, it will be the end of you," you say. "A beam of energy so bright, you'll frazzle."

The vampire snarls at you. "Perhaps so, but you'll never find out who my master is and what he wants with you..."

    ✣ *If you want to set off the grenade, go to 56.*
    ✣ *If you wish to find out who his master is, go to 62.*

37

You continue to make your way down the passageway. Rats scurry beneath your feet and water drips from the ceiling. The tunnel reeks with a putrid smell – the smell of fear and death, you think. Eventually you come to the end of the tunnel. A heavy-looking iron door blocks your way.

You turn the handle and find that the door isn't

locked. Taking a deep breath, you fling the door open and flatten yourself against the tunnel wall. Nothing happens. You decide to step inside. You enter the room – there are large electrical generators on the wall. You look up and give a gasp – there are hundreds of bats hanging from the ceiling!

As you stare at the sight, you hear the beating of wings – you have disturbed the creatures! One or two bats fly towards you screeching, instantly followed by more and more.

⸸ *To shoot at the bats, go to 64.*
⸸ *To get out of the room, go to 54.*

38

You run towards your gun, but as you bend down to pick it up, you hear a loud cracking noise. You look upwards. The last thing you see is a huge wooden beam falling on top of you. You scream in agony as your body is crushed. Then, mercifully, you sink into the darkness of oblivion. Like the vampire, you too will not leave this place alive.

⸸ *You have failed at the last hurdle, if you wish to begin again, go to 1.*

39

"Nothing you can say will interest me," you say coldly. As your finger tightens on the trigger, the vampire makes a supernatural leap at you.

You fire your gun, but miss. The vampire smashes its fist into your face and you drop down to the floor, unconscious.

‡ *Go to 70.*

40

Suddenly, a dark object comes flying out of the
doorway, smashing you in the chest. It knocks your
gun from your hand. You look down to see what hit
you and are puzzled – it is a leather bag. As you try
to regain your breath, a figure hurtles out of the room
and leaps at you – one of the vampires has survived!

The creature bares its fangs and knocks you to the
floor with the claws of its blistered hand. Its deadly
fangs are centimetres from your neck! You can smell
its putrid breath – it is the smell of death! With a

desperate twist of your body, you manage to throw it off, sending the creature sprawling across the floor. You both pick yourselves up and face each other in a battle to the death.

⸸ *To use your flamer, go to 83.*
⸸ *To fight it using your martial art skills, go to 98.*

41

You drop your gun and use your hands to chop at the vampire's head. The creature loses its grip on your throat and you break free.

You grasp for your gun – but it is too dark – you cannot see it. Again, you feel the vampire at your throat, you kick out desperately, and the creature releases you once more.

A voice from behind you turns your blood to ice. "I'm here to get you, Hunter, and there's nothing you can do to stop me!"

You realise that you are in a hopeless situation.

⸸ *Go to 98.*

42

You point your gun in the direction of the voice and pull the trigger.

"That wasn't very friendly, Hunter."

You let fly a volley of shots, spraying the room with wooden bullets. You stop shooting and look around the room, trying to see if you have hit your target.

Then from the silence, there is a sound of wings beating. In an instant a black-cloaked figure stands before you. The figure smiles, revealing a set of deadly looking fangs.

"Why don't you put your weapon down, Hunter? Then we can talk..."

‡ *If you want to try to shoot the vampire, go to 98.*
‡ *If you want to use the UV grenade, go to 56.*
‡ *If you wish to talk to the vampire, go to 55.*

43

You blast the lock with the flamer, heating up the metal. You test the door again and it snaps open.

You take out your gun and step cautiously inside. With your night-vision goggles on you can see several petrol cans on the floor. On the far wall there is a door, which is slightly open. A glow is coming from the room, which flares your night-vision and you can hear the murmur of voices.

‡ *If you wish to pick up one of the petrol cans and enter the room, go to 68.*

‡ *If you wish to refill your flamer before entering the room, go to 22.*

‡ *If you wish to return to the platform, go to 94.*

44

As you stand over the creature, the lobby is filled with the sound of beating wings. Hundreds of screeching bats appear and attack you. As you attempt to beat them off, you drop your gun.

The vampire cries out, "Brothers! Sisters! He is here!" In an instant several more figures emerge from the shadows. More bats fill the lobby, plunging it into blackness as you desperately try to fend them off and reach for your gun.

    † *To shoot at the bats, go to 64.*
    † *To shoot at the vampires, go to 46.*
    † *To try and escape, go to 54.*

45

You raise your gun and aim it at the creature's head. Just as you pull the trigger, it leaps towards you with unnatural speed and slams into your body, sending you sprawling backwards into a wall.

A bullet hits the cellar light, plunging the room into darkness.

At the same moment, the vampire is upon you. You feel its claw-like hands around your throat and can smell its foul breath.

"I can see you, but you can't see me," laughs the creature and tightens its grip on your throat.

  ‡ *If you wish to try and talk to the vampire,*
      go to 98.
  ‡ *If you wish to use your martial arts skills,*
      go to 41.

46

You blast one of the creatures and he explodes in a shower of ash.

The others scream and rush at you. You fight desperately to keep them off, but there are too many of them.

One of the vampires stands over you, fangs bared. "Brothers and sisters, it is feeding time," he cries.

  ‡ *Go to 98.*

47

You fire your gun and bullets rip into the creature's chest – but nothing else happens!

"Tut, tut, tut. You really should know that such weapons are useless against me," he laughs. "Soon your blood will mix with mine!" His hands tighten around your throat as he moves his fangs towards your neck.

- *If you wish to detonate the UV grenade, go to 56.*
- *If you wish to drop your gun and grab your flamer, go to 65.*
- *If you wish to fight and break free of the creature's grip, go to 99.*

48

As you turn away from the paydesk, you hear the sound of wings fluttering. You look up – the lobby is full of flying bats!

You spin around, the woman at the paydesk is snarling at you – her teeth are razor sharp – she is a vampire!

"Brothers, sisters – he is here!" In an instant several more figures emerge from the shadows.

More shrieking bats fill the lobby, diving at you as you desperately try to fend them off and reach for your gun. Then the lights go out.

- *To try and shoot at the bats, go to 64.*
- *To try and shoot at the vampires, go to 46.*
- *To try and escape, go to 54.*

49

With your night-vision goggles on, you make your
way down the winding set of stairs, gun at the ready.
You move carefully, watching out for traps, but there
are none, and no sign of the vampire.

Eventually you arrive at the bottom of the stairs.
There are two doors. One is open and has a sign
saying "Service Tunnel". The other door is shut and
has a painted warning on it: "DANGER – DO NOT
ENTER!" You try this door, but it is locked.

‡ *If you wish to blast the lock with your flamer,*
   go to 43.
‡ *If you choose to head into the tunnel, go to 6.*

50

Snow is still falling heavily as you arrive back at your
mansion. You drive through the large gateway, and
immediately know something is badly wrong. The
alarm system is wailing, but none of the security
lights are on. You park up the SUV and cautiously
approach the darkness of the main house, gun at the
ready. Activating your night-vision goggles, you can
see the door has been ripped from its hinges.

You enter the main door, step into the hallway
and take in the scene. Pictures have been torn off the

walls and cupboards have been emptied.

You begin a careful search of your house. Most rooms have been ransacked. You head upstairs and are checking your bedrooms when you hear a noise coming from the hallway. You make your way down the stairs. Both your study door and cellar door are swinging open – they hadn't been when you had gone upstairs. Someone, or something, is still in your house!

⁂ *If you wish to head down to the underground cellar, go to 12.*

⁂ *If you wish to check out the study, go to 66.*

50: Your mansion door lies in splinters.

51

You quietly open the door and step inside. The large room is lit by dozens of candles in silver candlesticks. Black and red silk curtains line the walls. You shiver with fear – the music is playing and you can still hear the chatter of voices, but there is no one in the room!

‡ *Go to 85.*

52

You walk back into the room. The scene is one of devastation. As you look on, you sense something

moving behind you. You swing round and dodge the attack, but as you do, your gun is smashed from your hand. One of the vampires has survived! Its hair has been burnt away and its skin is hanging off. Its jaws are open and it hisses at you with hatred.

"You have killed my brothers and sisters, you will suffer!" Its rage is all consuming. The creature slices at you with its clawed nails, tearing into your flesh. You try to block its attack, but the vampire is too powerful and it punches you to the floor.

You look up through blurred eyes and see a vision from your worst nightmares.

‡ *Go to 98.*

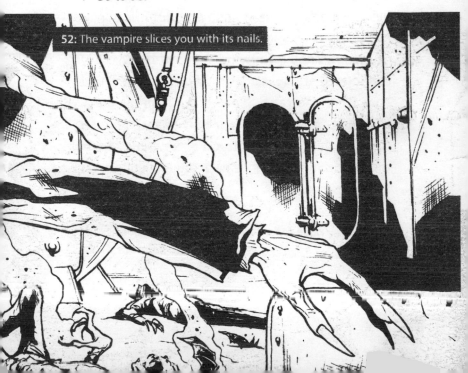

52: The vampire slices you with its nails.

53

Your finger rests on the trigger. "All right, tell me what I should know."

"Give me your word that you'll let me go, if I tell you," the creature says.

‡ *If you want to trick the vampire, go to 21.*
‡ *If you decide it is playing for time and you should shoot it, go to 39.*

54

You turn to escape, but the cloud of bats grows. The creatures begin to bite at you. Desperately, you try to pull them off your head and body, but it is hopeless – they overwhelm you.

You are smothered by hundreds of bats as they continue to attack you with their razor sharp teeth. Your skin is lacerated, blood pours from the hundreds of wounds. You scream helplessly as the creatures continue their frenzied attack. As your cries die out, their screeching becomes even louder, and you sink to the floor, dead.

‡ *You have failed. To begin again, return to 1.*

55

"Are you Mr Pavie?" you ask, as you lower your gun.

"That is one of my names, but perhaps it not the one I am generally known by," the creature replies. "You could say I am a little mixed up. Tell me, have you guessed my true name?" he asks.

‡ *If you've worked out Mr Pavie's true name, go to 36.*

‡ *If you don't know, go to 98.*

56

You pull out the UV grenade, and with a flick of your finger, detonate it. There is a roar and a blinding flash as UV rays fill the room. The light is intense – you try to shield your eyes, but you have made a mistake – you are in a confined space and the light instantly burns your retinas.

You scream in agony – you have blinded yourself. You hear the door open, and the thrilled screeches of vampires who have found their prey.

You can see nothing, but feel the pain as your flesh is ripped apart and you enter the world of darkness forever.

‡ *To restart your adventure, go to 1.*

57

You shoot the vampire quickly. With a demonic cry the creature turns to dust. You wait, ready to deal with any more creatures that might appear in response to the vampire's death cry. After a few tense minutes, nothing happens, so you decide to explore the building.

You look around the lobby and see a flight of stairs leading to the bowling alley and a door with a sign saying,

NO ADMITTANCE –
KNOCK 'EM DEAD STAFF ONLY.
YOU HAVE BEEN WARNED!

‡ *If you wish to try the door, go to 13.*
‡ *If you decide to head towards the bowling lanes, go to 88.*

58

It is still dark as you take off in your private jet. Soon you are heading into the night and you switch on the autopilot, giving you time to think about what has happened in the past few hours.

You wonder who Mr Pavie is and what the warnings you have been given mean. Why are you being sought – what do the vampires want with you?

Soon you are above Paris and take over the controls to land at a small airfield on the outskirts of the French capital.

You park up your jet and pick up the motorbike that is always kept for you at the airfield. You put on your helmet, type in the address of Mr Pavie's hotel into your satnav, kick-start the bike and drive into the centre of Paris.

You soon arrive at the Rue Morgue and park your bike outside the Hotel Paradise. You fling your bag of weapons over your shoulder and enter the hotel foyer – it is empty. You head towards the front desk and ring the bell. A receptionist steps out from a door. "*Bonjour, Monsieur,*" she says. "Can I help you?"

‡ *If you want to book a room, go to 14.*
‡ *If you wish to ask to see Mr Pavie, go to 31.*

59

As the vampire lunges forward, you reach for your gun and pull the trigger. The bullet hits the creature's arm and it staggers backwards. You fire again, missing its chest, but hitting it in the face. The vampire screams and turns away from its attack.

Through your night-vision goggles you see it changing into a bat. It flies towards the service tunnel stairway.

‡ *To keep shooting at the creature, go to 81.*
‡ *To follow it down the service tunnel stairway, go to 49.*

60

You pull out your gun and begin shooting at the vampires. One or two of the creatures fall to the ground, but there are too many of them. With a supernatural speed and strength they are upon you. You fumble for the trigger of the UV grenade, but then gasp in horror as it is knocked from your hand.

You continue to try and fight off the vampires, but it is hopeless. There are too many of them. Soon you are on your knees, held fast by the creatures of the night.

The old vampire moves towards you. He grins, revealing fangs that are flecked with blood. "You had a choice, Hunter, what a shame it is that you made the wrong one..."

‡ *Go to 99.*

61

You beat off the vampire's attack with a kick to his chest.

However, the vampire fights back and in the small confines of the elevator it is difficult to use your martial arts skills.

At the same time you feel a hand around your throat, tightening at your windpipe. Desperately you try to fight off the creature, but its grip is too strong. Slowly your airway is cut off and you slip into unconsciousness.

‡ *Go to 70.*

62

"Tell me who your master is, or I'll pull the trigger,"
you say. "And that'll be the end of you..."

In reply the creature laughs. "Catch me if you can.
Meet me at the Tower – if you dare!"

The vampire lets out a high-pitched scream. The
curtains fly back and the window glass shatters.
Before you can react, the creature turns into a bat
and flies out. You race over and see the bat flapping
its wings across the darkness of the Paris skyline,
heading towards the outline of the Eiffel Tower.

‡ *If you want to head up to the penthouse suite,*
go to 25.
‡ *If you wish to head to the Eiffel Tower, go to 75.*

63

Bats appear from nowhere, and as you race up the
stairs they crash into you, biting and scratching your
face. Still half-blinded, you stumble through the open
cellar door and slam it shut. Bats thud into the door
on the other side.

You decide to revisit the cellar, but only when you
have rearmed. Your eyes readjust to the gloom and
you head to the study.

‡ *Go to 66.*

64

In the darkness you shoot one or two bats, but there are too many and the creatures continue to swarm around you. Their high-pitched screeching is almost deafening!

Then, from the swirling black mass you see two piercing red eyes – the vampire you've been hunting has materialised in front of you!

‡ *To attack the vampire, go to 98.*
‡ *To try and escape, go to 54.*

65

You drop your gun and reach for your flamer. With a sharp movement, you pull the trigger and blast the vampire with a sheet of flame. His shirt catches fire and the creature staggers backwards. Quickly, you follow up with a kick to its chest. You notice that the vampire's cape is undamaged by the flames.

The vampire springs at you, knocking the flamer and the UV grenade from your hands. It rips off its burning shirt and claws at your body with its long talon-like fingers. You block its strikes and kick back at the vampire. As it moves to attack again you spin

to the side and manage to get the creature in a headlock. But the vampire transforms into a bat and you are left with just a cloak in your hands.

It flies towards the stairs and transforms back into its human form. "You cannot win, Hunter. Give up now and become a creature of the night."

"Don't you understand 'no' when you hear it?" you reply.

‡ *If you wish to detonate the UV grenade, go to 9.*
‡ *If you wish to continue to fight hand-to-hand, go to 98.*

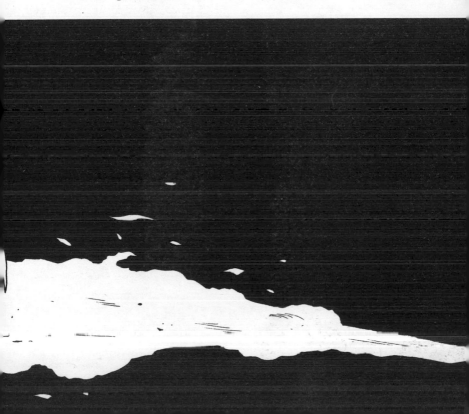

66

You enter the study. The doors leading to the garden are swinging open. You hurry towards them and step outside into the snow-filled air, but there is nothing or no one to be seen.

You step back inside the study and open a cupboard that contains a master control for the electricity supply. You flick a switch and the generators come to life, bringing electricity and light back to the mansion.

You turn on your desk lamp and see a letter lying on the desk, written in blood red ink. You read it.

Hunter

Well done! You have survived the brood in their lair at the underground station and the bowling alley. But there is more — if you wish to know about what the vampires are truly planning, you must go to Paris and visit a certain Mr Pavie. He knows all. He can be found in his suite at the Hotel Paradise on the Rue Morgue, Paris.

A. Friend

There is obviously more to this outbreak of vampires than you first thought! You decide to prepare for a trip to Paris.

☦ *Go to 29.*

67

You glance towards the receptionist's desk to check that you are not being watched before dashing up the stairs.

The penthouse suite is at the top of the building and you climb steadily upwards. As you get nearer the top of the staircase, the lights begin to flicker. You take out your gun, ready for any surprise attack and continue to make your way up the stairs.

After a few nerve-racking minutes, you arrive at a landing where you unpack the rest of your equipment: the flamer, the UV grenade and night-vision goggles.

There is another set of stairs on the left leading up to the penthouse suite, and on the right there is an unmarked door. You cup your ear to the door and can hear the chatter of voices and music being played.

‡ *If you wish to explore behind the door, go to 51.*
‡ *If you decide to turn away and carry on up the stairs, go to 95.*

68

You pick up a petrol can. It is full. You enter the room, gun at the ready. Before you is a group of a dozen or so down-and-outs, sitting in front of a small fire, which causes your night vision to flare and momentarily blind you. As your sight gradually returns, you see that the down-and-outs are staring at you.

"Who are you?" you ask. "And what are you doing down here?"

One of the men stands up. "Just a group of people fallen on hard times," he replies. "We mean no harm..."

You peer carefully at the man – there is something not quite right about him. As the other down-and-outs stand, you glance up and see that the roof is covered with bats, hanging upside down.

You look back at the group – they are smiling at you. You gasp. Their open mouths reveal their razor sharp fangs. Your stomach knots with fear – there isn't just one vampire – there's a whole brood of them!

One of the vampires leers at you. "Our master was expecting you..."

‡ *To shoot at the creatures, go to 46.*
‡ *To use the petrol can, go to 3.*
‡ *To run out of the room, go to 77.*
‡ *To use your martial arts skills, go to 98.*

69

You make your way back to the hotel. The receptionist seems surprised to see you, but you ignore her and head straight to the penthouse suite.

At the door you punch in the keycode you found on the mobile phone. Heavy bolts inside the door slide back and the door opens. You step inside and switch on the light. The room is all painted black and red. Gold ornaments and candlesticks line the shelves and tables.

You see that the walls are bare, except for a huge painting of a castle perched on the top of a mountain.

‡ *If you wish to examine the picture, go to 26.*
‡ *If you wish to examine the ornaments, go to 78.*

70

When you come round you find yourself tied to a chair. Several people, all dressed in black, are standing opposite you.

A tall man with long dark hair steps forward. "So the Hunter has been captured," he laughs. "You walked into our trap."

"What do you want with me?" you ask.

The man smiles, revealing his vampire teeth. "We want your blood. You are the Hunter, you have killed too many of our kind. Once you have become one of us, we will be safe. No one will be able to defeat us! My master will be the supreme ruler!"

You struggle, but the ropes are too tight. The vampire moves towards you. "Relax. There is no escape." He sinks his fangs into your neck. You feel your lifeblood being sucked away.

Hours later you regain consciousness. You are lying in a coffin. It is dark, but you can see perfectly and you have a craving for blood. In shock, you put your hand to your mouth and feel the sharp points of your teeth. You have become that which you once hunted – a vampire!

‡ *If you wish to begin again, go to 1.*

71

You stand over the writhing creature. "Who sent you here?" you ask.

The vampire just stares at you with hatred in its blood red eyes.

"Who is 'Mr Pavie'?" you continue.

The vampire laughs. "A name but not a name," replies the creature.

"What do you mean by that?" you ask.

"I will tell you nothing more – see you in hell."

You nod grimly. "As you wish. But you first!"

‡ *To use your flamer, go to 20.*
‡ *To shoot the vampire, go to 45.*

72

You drop from the platform and carefully make your way into the dark tunnel, making sure that you don't touch the deadly live rail track.

You walk further into the blackness. Stinking water drips from the ceiling and that familiar smell returns again. The smell of death is strong down here. Suddenly you freeze. You hear wings beating – lots of wings. Dark shapes flit through the tunnel, flicking your face, then scratching at your head. The bats rip off your night-vision goggles, plunging you into darkness. The air is filled with screeching bats. You realise you have disturbed an entire colony of them!

‡ *If you wish to walk back to the platform, go to 54.*
‡ *If you wish to shoot at the bats, go to 64.*

73

As blocks of stone and ceiling beams crash down, you run towards the fireplace and, with a great leap, launch yourself at the picture of the castle above it.

Once again, there is a maelstrom of noise and wind and you feel yourself spinning and spinning around like a leaf in the wind.

‡ *Go to 100.*

74

Carefully, you climb up the icy metal steps. Halfway up the fire escape, there is an open window. Through it is a corridor leading towards a flight of stairs.

‡ *If you want to climb in through the window, go to 24.*
‡ *If you wish to continue climbing up the steps to the roof, go to 35.*

75

You head out of the hotel and start up your motorbike. You pull back the throttle and hurtle through the snow-filled roads of Paris. You arrive at the Eiffel Tower. It is still before dawn when you arrive at the deserted tower.

You park your motorbike, pick up your bag of equipment and head to one of the four great pylons. You look upwards – outlined in the full moon, you can see a cloud of bats flying around. You are sure that Mr Pavie is at the top of the tower, waiting for you – but what will be the best way to reach him?

You look around and consider your options. There is a set of stairs and an elevator – or you could climb up the steel pylons.

‡ *If you wish to climb up the stairs, go to 91.*
‡ *If you want to take the elevator, go to 17.*
‡ *If you wish to climb up the steel pylons, go to 80.*

76

You remove your goggles. Your eyes are still blurry but you can see well enough to get out of the cellar. Even with the light on now, you can't see the bats but you can hear them. Someone, or something, must have

reactivated the switches at the electricity fuse box in the cellar to turn the lights on.

‡ *To explore the cellar further, go to 5.*
‡ *If you want to leave the cellar and explore the study upstairs, go to 63.*

77

Before you can escape from the room, one of the vampires shouts out, "Kill!"

The air becomes filled with hundreds of shrieking bats. The creatures smash into your head and attack your face. They rip the night-vision goggles from your face, plunging you into near darkness.

‡ *To shoot the bats with your gun, go to 64.*
‡ *If you still wish to leave the room, go to 54.*

78

Suddenly, you hear a fluttering sound coming from behind you. You spin around and see a cloud of bats swarming towards you. In an instant, you are smothered by the screeching creatures.

‡ *Go to 54.*

78: A cloud of madly-flapping bats engulfs you.

79

You smile at the woman. "There's just one more thing..." You reach for your gun and aim it at her head. "Where are the rest of you?"

The woman snarls and bares her sharp teeth – you were right to be suspicious of her, it is a vampire! It leaps at you, but you easily avoid the creature's attack and knock it to the ground.

‡ *If you decide to shoot the vampire, go to 57.*
‡ *If you want to interrogate it, go to 44.*

80

You begin to climb up the steel pylons of the tower using the rivets as footholds. The ice and snow make the climb treacherous. Several times you nearly lose your footing. Higher and higher you climb, until you are halfway up the tower.

Suddenly, a dark shape flits in front of you, followed by another and another. A cloud of bats swarm at you, covering your body and biting at you. Their sharp teeth rip into your skin. You desperately flail at them, but it is hopeless, their relentless attack continues.

Your grip loosens on the steel girders and you slip – losing your hold. Screaming, you plunge downwards

towards the ground below. You hit the concrete with
a sickening thud and your screams are cut off forever.

> ⸸ *You have failed. If you wish to begin again,*
> *return to 1.*

81

You continue firing, but the creature is too fast and
it disappears into the blackness of the stairway. You
reload your gun.

> ⸸ *If you wish to follow it, go to 49.*
> ⸸ *If you wish to take the stairs to the platform,*
> *go to 90.*

82

Just as you are about to sneak out through the door,
a black-cloaked figure with an evil smile steps in front
of you.

"Hello, Hunter – leaving so soon?" The creature
grins, revealing a set of deadly pointed fangs.

You reach into your bag and pull out your gun, but
with supernatural speed, the vampire springs across
the room, slamming into you and knocking the air
from your body and the gun from your hand.

You stagger back to your feet, spin around and with a perfectly executed roundhouse kick, you smash the creature's face open. It emits a nightmarish scream, and resumes its attack. You fight back, but the vampire is powerful and counters your every move. As your strength weakens, it flies across at you, sending you crashing into the stone wall. You slump to the ground and the vampire pins you to the floor, before gripping your throat with its long claw-like hands.

You struggle desperately, but you cannot fight it off – its hands tighten on your throat – you are unable to breathe! You quickly slip into unconsciousness.

‡ *Go to 70.*

83

The vampire runs towards you, arms outstretched, teeth bared. With one movement you grab your flamer, aim it and blast the vampire's head. With a roar, the creature is engulfed in flames and crashes to the floor.

As the flames consume the creature of the night, it screams at you. "Enjoy this victory, Hunter. My master will have revenge. More will follow – we want your blood and will have it. Your days are numbered."

You pick up your gun. "Not as numbered as yours

– goodbye, sucker," you say and fire a bullet into its heart. The vampire instantly dissolves into dust.

Wondering what the vampire threw at you, you return to the object. It is a leather bag; inside is a ten-pin bowling ball and a card:

KNOCK 'EM DEAD
BOWLING ALLEY
WHITECHAPEL, LONDON

You are puzzled as to what a vampire would have to do with a bowling alley. You decide to investigate.

‡ *Go to 8.*

84

Before you can escape from the room, one of the vampires shouts out, "Kill!"

The air is suddenly filled with hundreds of shrieking, bloodthirsty bats.

+ *If you still wish to get out of the room, go to 54.*
+ *If you decide to take on the vampires after all, go to 4.*

85

You walk further into the room and the door slams behind you. Suddenly there is a supernatural blast of wind, which turns into howling laughter. The silk curtains flap wildly and the voices and music cease.

Holding your gun you spin around, but can see no one. The hairs on your neck begin to stand on end – you can sense danger. Cautiously, you move further into the room, ready for whatever might come.

Then out of the darkness, a lone voice echoes around the room. "Welcome, Hunter. Welcome to the lair of Mr Pavie. And what brings you here, I wonder?"

+ *If you want to reply, go to 55.*
+ *If you wish to fire your gun, go to 42.*

86

Struggling against the rush of wind, you continue along the tunnel. The roaring sound is almost deafening. Bright lights fill the tunnel – blinding you.

Realisation suddenly hits you: a train is hurtling towards you! You turn to run, but you are too slow. There is a screech of brakes as the driver sees you and tries to stop the train, but it is too late. The train smashes into your body, splintering your bones and sending you to oblivion.

⸭ *Your adventure has ended. To start again, turn back to 1.*

87

Still holding the grenade, you pull out your gun and begin shooting. One-by-one the vampires fall, victims to your deadly aim.

You move across the hall at speed, picking off the monstrous creatures until all except the Master vampire are dead. He has not moved, he is still standing on the staircase staring at you with hatred.

"So much for your brood," you say. "It's just me and you, now."

With a savage snarl, the vampire flies towards you at lightning speed and before you can react, its clawed hands reach for your throat.

‡ *To shoot the vampire, go to 47.*
‡ *To detonate the grenade, go to 56.*
‡ *To use your flamer, go to 65.*

88

The stairs lead to the bowling lanes. You can hear the dull thud of bowling balls and the clatter of pins being knocked down.

You put your weapon into your bag and enter the bowling hall. There are about half a dozen people bowling. One or two of them glance at you. Two members of staff, a woman and a man, are standing behind a refreshment counter.

You head to the counter. Before you can order anything the man speaks. "We were expecting you..."

You suddenly realise that the sounds of bowling have stopped. You turn and see the group of bowlers heading towards you. Some are holding bowling pins and balls. They smile, revealing their deadly fangs. More vampires!

You sigh. "You creatures are becoming a real pain in the neck!"

⚰ *If you decide there are too many of them to fight, go to 84.*

⚰ *If you decide to take them on, go to 4.*

89

Despite the blinding glare from the lights you fire
your gun several times.

You can hardly see and the gunshots seem to have
no effect on the bats as they fly at you, their tiny
wingtips brushing against your cheeks and their small
bodies crashing into your body.

You try to brush them away, but there are more
and more of them, screeching as they continue with
their attack.

‡ *To turn and run up the steps, go to 54.*
‡ *If you wish to keep shooting as you try to get
out, go to 34.*

90

With your gun at the ready, you carefully make your
way down the stairway. Even with your night-vision
goggles on, the shadows are unnaturally dark. You
listen for any sound that might give away the location
of the vampire. However, there is nothing but silence.

You finally reach the platform. Rats scamper across
the floor and a stale, familiar smell fills your nostrils
– death. In front of you is the train track heading into
two tunnels at either end of the platform. A sign on
the wall says: "WARNING – LIVE TRACK". You look

around the platform and see an old vending machine ripped open. You grab the broken door and drop it on the track. There is a loud bang and a huge flash of light that nearly throws you off your feet and blinds you temporarily. You realise that although the station is abandoned, the track is still used and has a deadly electric current passing through it!

- ‡ *If you wish to make your way down the left-hand tunnel, go to 27.*
- ‡ *If you wish to make your way down the right-hand tunnel, go to 72.*
- ‡ *If you wish to explore the platform, go to 19.*

91

You race up the metal stairs and soon reach the first floor of the tower.

Heart pounding, you continue up to the next level of the tower. You quickly reach it, but then realise that there are no more steps up the tower – you will have to get up to the top another way.

- ‡ *If you wish to take the elevator, go to 17.*
- ‡ *If you decide to climb up the elevator cable, go to 11.*
- ‡ *If you wish to climb up the pylons, go to 80.*

92

The vampires continue their attack, but your fighting skills are too good for them. Soon there is only one of the creatures left standing. You aim your gun at the creature's head.

As you are about to pull the trigger, the vampire holds its hands up in surrender. "Don't shoot," it says. "I have some information that you should know."

‡ *If you want to listen to the vampire, go to 53.*
‡ *If you decide to shoot it, go to 39.*

93

You run to the huge iron door and try to pull it open. You heave at it, but it is hopeless – it is locked! The castle is still falling apart. The staircase splits in half and huge blocks of stone crash down around you.

‡ *If you want to try and shoot the lock, go to 38.*
‡ *If you wish to head for the fireplace, go to 73.*

94

Before you can turn, a dark shape bursts through the door and leaps at you.

More dark figures rush through the door and grab

at you. You struggle desperately, but there are too many of them. Within seconds you are overpowered.

A tall figure steps from the throng of people that surround you. It is the vampire you've been hunting!

"You foolish human," he says. "Say hello to my followers, for you are going to become one of them." He opens his mouth, revealing his deadly fangs.

‡ *Go to 98.*

95

Holding your gun ready, you make your way up the stairs. The lights flicker as you climb higher. You can feel your heart beating faster and your breathing becomes shallower.

Eventually you reach the top of the stairs and see a solid-looking steel door that evidently leads to the penthouse suite. There is an access keypad on the right-hand side. You groan in frustration – entering a wrong access code could set off a warning alarm, and even with your flamer you know you won't be able to blast the door open. You look around to see if there is any other means of entry, but there isn't. You decide that you will have to explore the room below.

‡ *Go to 51.*

96

You leave your SUV and head down a snow-covered alleyway at the side of the building.

You see a door marked KNOCK 'EM DEAD STAFF. Further along the alley is a metal fire escape leading up to the roof of the building. Its steps are covered in ice.

‡ *If you wish to return to the front entrance, go to 30.*
‡ *If you wish to try the door, go to 13.*
‡ *If you wish to climb up the fire escape, go to 74.*

97

You stand at the top of the steps to the light-flooded cellar. Gun ready, you make your way down the stone steps. You hear wings beating the air and you see the shadow of a bat fly across the cellar.

There is another fluttering of wings and in the light you can make out the shape of dozens of tiny bats, hanging from the ceiling. The air is suddenly filled with an ear-splitting high-pitched screech, causing you to grimace in pain. Then as if acting on an order, the creatures suddenly begin to fly at you.

‡ *If you wish to use the UV grenade, go to 56.*
‡ *If you wish to ignore the bats and move further into the cellar, go to 16.*

98

In an instant the vampire is at your throat. Its sharp teeth rip into your neck. You try desperately to fight off the creature, but it is hopeless. The creature throws back its head and gives a cry of bloodlust and triumph. You feel the lifeblood being sucked out of your body. Soon, you too will become a creature of the night.

‡ *You have failed. To begin again, turn back to 1.*

99

"The hunt is over for you," rasps the creature. "You have killed too many of our kind. Once you have become one of us, we will be safe. The Hunter's blood mixed with that of the vampire! We will be invincible! No one will be able to defeat us!" The vampire sinks his fangs into your neck. You feel your lifeblood being sucked away.

Hours later you regain consciousness. It is dark, but you can see perfectly. You are lying in a coffin and you have a craving for blood. You put your hand to your mouth and feel the sharp points of your teeth. You have become that which you once hunted – a vampire!

‡ *If you are brave enough to begin your adventure again, go to 1.*

100

The noise and wind stop and you find yourself back in the penthouse suite.

You look at the picture on the wall and smile as you watch the castle collapse to the ground. You take one of the lit candles and set fire to the picture.

Soon it is a pile of ashes, like so many of the vampires you have killed. Nothing will be coming in through that gateway to the otherworld, you think to yourself. With a last glance at the destroyed picture, you head towards the door.

You have succeeded this time, but there will be more supernatural creatures that you will have to deal with, of that there is no doubt. But for now, your hunt is over. You step through the doorway and head for home.

About the 2Steves

⚓ Steve Barlow and Steve Skidmore have been writing together for over twenty years. Known as the 2Steves, they have written over 125 books together. Visit www.the2steves.net

Steve Barlow

⚓ Born: Crewe, UK
⚓ Description: Tall and hairy
⚓ Most horrific job: Emptying rubbish bins
⚓ Most horrific pet: Igor the cannibal gerbil
⚓ Favourite horror creature: Mothra – I just love the idea of a gigantic moth that destroys whole cities!
⚓ Favourite horror film: *An American Werewolf in London*

Steve Skidmore

⚓ Born: Leicester, UK
⚓ Description: Short and less hairy than Barlow
⚓ Most horrific job: Counting pastry pie lids
⚓ Most horrific pet: A mad rabbit
⚓ Favourite horror creature: Vampire
⚓ Favourite horror film: *The Omen*

Steve Barlow

iHorror: the story so far...

 We came up with the idea for iHorror after writing I HERO, a series of interactive books for Franklin Watts, a children's publisher. The series features books where you become the hero, such as a gladiator or a spy or an astronaut, and decide what happens in the adventure. With iHorror, we wanted to do something much scarier!

 That's right. Because we love scary stuff! And we don't think nice girls should fall in love with vampires because they're tragically misunderstood. Vampires really aren't very nice creatures, and iHorror is designed for people who'd rather kill the bloodsucking creeps than kiss them!

 So iHorror was born. But these aren't ordinary books – which you'll already know if you've read one of the I HERO titles. They are also more difficult to write than "normal" books – we have to do research, planning, more planning, writing, drawing spider diagrams to link all the paragraphs up, more writing, and then the editing starts.

 And that's when the reader takes over and decides how the story will work out!

Steve Skidmore

Interview with the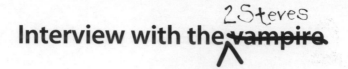

‡ So, Steve B why choose to write about vampires?

 Because they are scary things – creatures of the night with bloodsucking fangs and the ability to change shape. There aren't many things that are more horrible! If you take one out to dinner, what's on the menu will probably be you! Order something with lots of garlic and if the waiter asks you what sort of water you'd like, sparkling or still, say "Holy"...

‡ Steve S, what was the hardest part of Vampire Hunter to write?

 It has to be the actual planning of the book – how to join up all the different episodes and make sure that it fits together. Actually thinking up all the horrific things that can happen is easy! Making them fit together is hard!

‡ Steve B, how do you go about writing stories together?

 We do a lot of talking and planning before we ever begin to write. And, no, we don't argue...

Yes, we do.

 No, we don't!

 Yes, we do... (actually, we don't really!)

⚉ Steve S, who comes up with the ideas for all the fantastic weapons?

 We both do! We talk about which weapons are best to get rid of vampires – technology has moved on, so we don't rely on the old-fashioned stake through the heart nonsense.

⚉ Finally, Steve B, can you tell me who the Hunter is? (Go on, I promise not to tell.)

 Everyone who reads these books is the Hunter. It could even be you...

⚉ Really? Well thanks for writing such great books – I hope everyone enjoys them!

Creating the artwork of iHorror

The inside artwork for iHorror is drawn by Paul Davidson. We've put together some pieces to show you the stages of progression. Below is the scene from paragraph 11, when Mr Pavie confronts the Hunter at the Eiffel Tower. Paul says: "You can really see how the inking process gives a piece like this lots of impact. Here we've merged the rough pencil and ink final alongside each other."

"Here you can see subtle changes from the pencil rough, including the main vampire's wider eyes."

"This piece of the Master vampire really came to life once it had been inked."

"A rough pencil sketch of the Hunter, one of the different poses chosen. This one isn't in the competition – see the last page for details."

Paul says: "This is the art for paragraph 3. I had to add a bit more space in the middle because of the gutter (the fold in the middle of the two pages)."

"'Mr Pavie' appears... I love drawing vampires!"

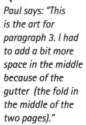

"Here the rough was approved, but there was still a lot of work to do. All the structural iron on the tower and the perspective meant this piece took about 5 hours to finish."

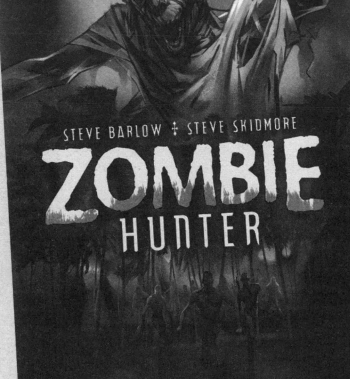

You have been contacted by Mr Romero Price, head of the Nutco Oil Corporation. His company is based on the South Pacific islands of Saruba and Panuka. Saruba is well known to you. For hundreds of years tales from the island have told of the dead rising up out of their freshly dug graves in the form of zombies. But you've never actually been to Saruba. These living dead creatures are difficult to destroy and will not stop hunting for living flesh to feed on.

Mr Price claims that zombies are now highly active on Saruba, which is affecting Nutco's ability to harvest the nut crop grown on the island and processes it into oil. As you are the world's expert at dealing with zombies, he has promised to pay you a substantial sum of money to destroy the zombies on the island and to find out where they are coming from. Of course, you have accepted the challenge and are looking forward to once again fighting the creatures of the supernatural.

You have packed the weapons and equipment you think you will need to destroy the zombies, and have flown your private jet to the South Pacific.

There is nowhere to land your jet on Saruba, so you fly to the airport on the neighbouring island of Panuka. Your request for permission to land is granted. But the descent is a bumpy one. Dark storm clouds are gathering as you approach the runway – lightning flashes across the sky and you wonder if this is an omen of what is to come...

‡ *Go to 1.*

1

Heavy rain lashes down as you land your jet and taxi towards the arrivals building. You bring the jet to a halt, power down the engines and open the door. As you descend the steps with your bags, a tall man approaches you, holding out one hand, and carrying a large umbrella in the other. You are surprised to see that, despite the pouring rain, he is wearing sunglasses.

The man introduces himself as a representative of Nutco Oil. "Mr Price has sent me to collect you. He is very anxious to meet you," he says in a strangely slurred and hollow voice. "Nutco's HQ is in the hills of Panuka, so we'll be flying there by helicopter. Please come this way."

He helps to carry your bags to the waiting helicopter through the pouring rain. You stow all of your bags except your case of weapons. You slide this on to the rear seat next to you, put on the helicopter's communication headphones and settle down to enjoy the ride. The man takes his seat in the front and fires up the helicopter's engine.

Soon you are in the air and heading towards the HQ. The weather is getting worse – visibility is limited and lightning crackles across the sky, buffeting the helicopter.

"Do you think we should turn back?" you say to the

pilot through your communication mic.

The pilot shakes his head. "Relax – just take it easy. This is going to be the ride of your life – or rather, your death!" He turns round, takes off his glasses and gives you a skull-like grin. Your stomach lurches as you stare into two pus-filled, maggoty eyes – the pilot is a zombie! He laughs manically and thrusts downwards on the controls, sending the helicopter diving towards the ground.

‡ *If you wish to fight using your martial arts skills, go to 11.*

‡ *If you wish to use your flame gun, go to 75.*

‡ *If you wish to shoot the zombie, go to 29.*

TO BE CONTINUED IN
     iHORROR: ZOMBIE HUNTER...

iHorror

STEVE BARLOW ✦ STEVE SKIDMORE

WEREWOLF HUNTER

Fight your fear. Choose your fate...

978 1 40830 987 2   PB   £4.99

A full moon hangs high in the sky, casting an evil glow. Werewolves are on the prowl for flesh, gathering in numbers and strength. You must track these inhuman creatures across North America to fight face-to-face with the pack leader before time runs out and the Great Hunt begins. Go now! Stop the rampage of the werewolves in its tracks.

The Japanese island of Okinawa is rocked by a massive earthquake – opening a fiery portal to the underworld! Terrible demons flood through, bent on tormenting humankind and making Earth a living nightmare. Only you can stand up to these unearthly horrors. Only you can send them back to the depths where they belong.

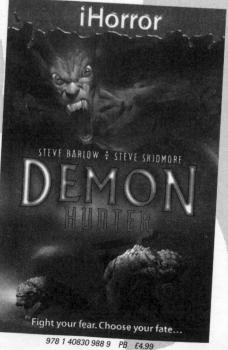

iHorror

STEVE BARLOW ✦ STEVE SKIDMORE

DEMON HUNTER

Fight your fear. Choose your fate...

978 1 40830 988 9   PB   £4.99

9781408313886 PB £5.99

His lungs were gone. He was completely hollow inside.
But he was not dead. Not quite.

What happens when Robin Hood and his Merry Men are
faced with a plague of zombies? Somehow, Robin must
figure out a way to defeat the most difficult and
dangerous enemy he's ever faced, and save the
country from destruction...

ORCHARD BOOKS
www.orchardbooks.co.uk